Final Edition

www.finaleditiononline.com

Volume I № 1   Autumn 2004 • US $10

Contents

Editor in Chief:
Wallace Shawn
Managing Editor:
Jennifer Mahlman
Publishers:
Wallace Shawn, Inc.
& Seven Stories Press

Special Thanks:

Anthony Arnove
Christopher Black
Brenda Coughlin
Max Fenton
Libby Titus
Patty Woo

ISBN: 1-58322-684-2

Seven Stories Press
140 Watts Street
New York, NY 10013
www.sevenstories.com

From the Editor

Most of the writers who appear in this magazine live in New York. We all are "Americans." We all live in the United States. And we have to think about being American, because this is a very unusual moment in the history of this country or any country.

A few months ago, the American public, who in political theory and to some extent even in reality are "sovereign" in the United States, were given a group of pictures showing American soldiers tormenting desperate, naked, extremely thin people in chains— degrading them, mocking them, and physically torturing them. And so the question arose, How would the American public react to that? And the answer was that in their capacity as individuals, certain people definitely suffered or were shocked when they saw those pictures. But in their capacity as the sovereign public, they did not react. A cry of lamentation and outrage did not rise up across the land. The president and his highest officials were not compelled to abase themselves publicly, apologize, and resign, nor did they find themselves thrown out of office, nor did the political candidates from the party out of power grow hoarse with denouncing the astounding crimes which were witnessed by practically everyone throughout the entire world. As far as one could tell, over a period of weeks, the atrocities shown in the pictures had been assimilated into the list of things which the American public was willing to consider normal and which they could accept. And so now one has to ask, Well, what does that portend? And so we have to think about being Americans and living in the United States.

To be absolutely frank, the words "The United States" are not interesting to me, and I would much rather think about something else and talk about something else. Life is shockingly short even for those who live to be a hundred, and I'd rather spend my time listening to Schoenberg's incredibly gorgeous "Book of the Hanging Gardens" song cycle than thinking about the activities of men in

Washington D.C. who have a sick need to set fire to cities, wear enormous crowns, and march across crowds of prostrate people. In a way I find those men very, very boring, but the problem is that *they* would say that all of the marching and trampling they're doing is actually for the benefit of me and everyone I know, and unfortunately I have to admit that that actually is true. It's simply true, certainly in regard to me. I lead a very easy life and a very pleasant life, thanks to the oil and other supplies that these boring and unappealing men have collected and delivered to my apartment. So I'm up to my neck in being an American, whether I like it or not.

Of course I *don't* like it, because I don't feel a loyalty to this or any other particular place, apart from our very beautiful planet. It's not about the United States. Yes, the United States was created through a genocide, but on the other hand the United States has always had some absolutely wonderful characteristics. The United States is what it is. I don't love it, and I don't un-love it. The point is only that I'm not a believer in nation-states, passports, or immigration laws, and I don't think it's more important for an American to have a job than for a Guatemalan to have a job, and I don't value an American life more than I value a Nigerian life. I just happen to have been born here. That's it. Well, and then I stayed here—in large part because New York City felt actually like a somewhat thrilling microcosm of the world to me—part of one country, part of the United States, yet not really.

In confusing times and bad times, it seems natural to collect around oneself a group of friends and people one trusts, to try to figure things out. So that's what this is. It's not going to be an institution, because I don't think everything has to be an institution, and sometimes the impulse to make things permanent can be a symptom of the grandiosity that is part of our problem. So that's why this magazine is going out of business after its first issue and has therefore been given the name FINAL EDITION.

—WALLACE SHAWN
New York City
October 1, 2004

3

Invitation to a Degraded World

by Jonathan Schell

Ever since September 11, 2001, and the "war on terror" it occasioned, the very quality of public events—their grain, their tenor, their style, if you like—has seemed to undergo a certain deterioration, as if from that day forward history was being authored by a third-rate writer rather than a master, or was being compelled, even as it visited increasing suffering on real people, to follow the plot of a bad comic book. Not the representation of the events but the actual events, not the renderings of the characters involved but those characters themselves, not the telling of the story but the story itself—all seem to have become crasser, coarser, woven of shoddier materials. The tone was perhaps set by the sudden appearance of Osama bin Laden,

4

a mass murderer who came across at the same time as a comic-book, caricature villain—a man whom it would be impossible to take seriously if he had not killed so many people. The plan that he brought to fruition on September 11 was lifted whole out of any number of action comics, video games, or disaster movies, most of which end up with buildings blowing up, the more the better. (For example, in the most recent Terminator movie, *The Rise of the Machines*, starring the current governor of California, scarcely any standing structure shown on camera survives for more than a few minutes, and the movie winds up with a nuclear holocaust.) Bin Laden's choice of spectacle obviously was contrived to match this stock scene. He lacked any capacity to even slightly dent the military power of the United States, so he delivered his blow to the nation's psyche instead. What better means than to turn its most common fantasies into horrifying life? He was assisted in his aim by accident. The towers had been designed to withstand airplane crashes. Perhaps that's why, immediately after the attack, the authorities in New York failed to give timely warning that the towers might come down. Yet they did come down, and when they did the emotional power of the catastrophe was magnified a hundred-fold. The attacks alone would have been an event of the first order; but it was the belief-defying, heart-crushing fall of the towers that knocked history off its course. (What would the world be like now if the girders holding up the buildings had managed to withstand the fires? Would there have been a Camp X-ray in Guantánamo, a war in Iraq, a global "war on terror"?)

As it was, the towers' collapse added an element of the uncanny to the fantasy made real by bin Laden. Yet although the scale of the crime was new, his strategy was hardly original. Terrorists have long compensated for their military weakness by creating the greatest possible spectacle with their bloody acts. They work in a symbolic realm. Real destruction and real deaths are only the means to accomplish their psychological effects. It's a strategy that cannot succeed without the de facto cooperation of the news media, which are routine exploiters for commercial purposes of all varieties of violence and destruction, from the local murder or fire in the warehouse to the latest hurricane. (How often does a meeting of negotiators, or a city council or parliament lead the news?) Their habits have guaranteed that the terrorists get all the coverage they hope for. These media have in addition been busy in recent years scrambling reality and fantasy for entertainment purposes. A watershed was the coverage of the car chase in which the Los Angeles police pursued the white Bronco carrying O.J. Simpson, fleeing arrest for the alleged murder of his wife. Like the September 11 attacks, the Simpson episode recreated in the real world a type of scene—in this instance, the car-chase—that had been seen endlessly in movies and on television. What was sensational in the event was not any intrinsic drama (all you could see were a couple of cars driving along a highway) but the fact that the stale fictional scene was being lived out by real people. Ghoulish criminal cases, always popular, soon became the main stock-in-trade of television news—infotainment. Soon came "reality" television, which reversed the process of the Simpson chase. If infotainment started with real events and turned them into de facto soap operas, reality television started with soap operas and spiced them up by adding "real" elements (consisting mostly of people being serially kicked off the shows).

It goes without saying that movie mayhem and reality television have no moral likeness to September 11. However, the news media's longstanding symbiosis with violent criminals along with their infection of reality with fantasy provided models for bin Laden's action as well as a global stage on which it would appear and be guaranteed unlimited coverage. Bin Laden strove for maximum effect with his crime, and he was granted it. At the time, it seemed that everyone was saying or writing, "Everything has changed." (I also wrote it, in a column right after the attack.) But in this reaction, felt as defiance of bin Laden, was there not also a kind of *surrender*—not, to be sure, exactly to him, but to his debased style of thinking, his understanding of how the world works? What was damaged was not only the quality of political discussion and decision-making but something that might be called the dignity of the real. Surely our reaction suited bin Laden well. He had no power to "change everything" unless the government of the United States agreed. *Then* everything *could* change.

The government of the United States did agree. And a lot of things—if not everything—did change. President Bush seemed to accept bin Laden's invitation to enter into the world of an apocalyptic comic book. Even today, it may be hard to think of any response to September 11 as excessive. A great atrocity had been committed. A great reaction was needed. But was it necessary or wise to divide every person and government on earth into two camps—the good, the lovers of freedom, who are "with us," and the "evil-doers" who hate the good ones for their very goodness, and "who are against us?"—as if no other evils or horrors existed on earth to compel the attention of human beings? The comic-book aspect became even more pronounced when the president turned himself into a sort of real life action figure, donning a pilot's suit and landing on the deck of the USS *Abraham Lincoln* to declare success in the Iraq war (though in his National Guard service, in which he was trained as a pilot, he was grounded for failing to show up for a physical). But the fullest realization of a fantasy world built on the foundation of September 11 was the Republican convention, where a collection of villains abroad were blurred into one mass of evil-doers who were in turn blurred with John Kerry, depicted as their domestic accomplice. Iraq, descending in actuality into anarchy, was presented as an inspiring example of democracy for the entire Middle East. Hidden behind the visions of a glorious future—the favorite tense of the demagogue—rose the pile of corpses, Iraqi and American. It was a further curious demonstration of the power of the illusion that, as it developed, bin Laden himself slipped through the administration's fingers, as if the actual villain of September 11 had been dissolved in the fantasy his act set in motion.

Each country that plunges into nightmare—whether Germany under Hitler, the Soviet Union under the Bolsheviks, Chile under Pinochet, or, for that matter, Iraq under Saddam Hussein—travels there along its own path. The American political system—based on free elections, the rights of citizens, and the rule of law—is, though under the severest pressure, still available for use. If it is lost, and the full American nightmare descends, there will be many causes. They will include the militarization of foreign policy, global imperial ambition, the loss of balance among the branches of government, the erosion of civil liberties, and the overwhelming influence of corporate money and power over political life—all present before Osama bin Laden made his appearance. But at every step of the way the skids will be greased by the national capacity, conferred by the media and exploited by politicians, to produce and consume illusion, which, though hardly an American monopoly, may be the specific form of corruption most dangerous to American democracy. Once, observers imagined that we were entering an information age, but they were wrong. It is a misinformation age. The stupendous machinery of modern media has reached into every cranny of American life. Its outlets have been posted in every household, like a mechanical standing army. The steady, mild propaganda of advertising has long saturated the home for hours every day, the mental equivalent of low-level radiation. Now the public is being dosed with more virulent stuff. The standing army has been given increasingly insistent political marching orders. Stalin and Mao, confined mainly to radios and megaphones, could only dream of such penetration of daily life by their propaganda apparatuses. The injection of fantasy into the real offends the aesthetic sense, but the true price is paid in blood—in the torture of prisoners, in the launch of wars. If a grasp of reality and the constitutional machinery to act upon it remain intact, then every other ill can be addressed. But if these are lost, the capacity to recover is lost with it, and the game is over.

Interview with Noam Chomsky

by Wallace Shawn

TIME: September 17, 2004

PLACE: Chomsky's office in the Department of Linguistics and Philosophy at M.I.T.

WS: A lot of what you've written has to do with the ways in which human beings use their minds—use their very capacity for rationality, one could say—not to seek truth, but on the contrary to distort truth—to twist truth, often so as to justify various crimes they want to commit or have already committed. And this doesn't have to do so much with our personal behavior but with our behavior in groups. So-called leaders dream up the justifications, and everybody else absorbs and accepts them.

NC: It's simply very easy to subordinate oneself to a worldview that's supportive of one's own interests. Most of us don't go around murdering people or stealing food from children. There are a lot of activities that we just regard as pathological when we do them individually. On the other hand, when they're done collectively, they're considered necessary and appropriate. Clinton, Kennedy: they all carried out mass murder, but they didn't think that that was what they were doing—nor does Bush. You know, they were defending justice and democracy from greater evils. And in fact I think you'd find it hard to discover a mass murderer in history who didn't think that. . . . It's kind of interesting to read the Russian archives, which are coming out now. They're being sold, like everything in Russia, and so we're learning something about the internal discussions of the Russian leaders, and they talked to each other the same way they talked publicly. I mean, these gangsters, you know, who were taking over Eastern Europe in the late '40s and early '50s—they were talking to each other soberly about how we have to defend East European democracy from the fascists who are trying to undermine it. It's pretty much the public rhetoric, and I don't doubt that they believed it.

WS: But one has to say about human beings—well, human beings did manage to invent the concepts of truth and falsity, and that's a remarkable accomplishment. And surely if people really used the concepts of truth and falsity rigorously, if they applied the laws of rationality rigorously, they would be forced to confront the true nature of the things they might be planning to do, and that might be enough to prevent them from doing many terrible things.

After all, most justifications for mass murder flatly contradict the perpetrator's professed beliefs—and are based on factually false assumptions as well. Couldn't education somehow lead people to use their capacity for rational thought on a more regular basis, to take rationality more seriously? So that they *couldn't* accept absurd justifications for things? As we're sitting here in the Department of Linguistics and Philosophy, wouldn't it benefit the world if more people studied philosophy?

NC: Take Heidegger, one of the leading philosophers of the twentieth century. I mean, just read his straight philosophical work, "Introduction To Metaphysics." A few pages in, it starts off with the Greeks, as the origins of civilization, and the Germans as the inheritors of the Greeks, and we have to protect the Greek heritage. . . . This was written in 1935. The most civilized people in the West, namely the Germans—Germany was the most educated country in the world—the Germans were coming under the delusion that their existence, and in fact the existence of Western Civilization since the Greeks, was threatened by fierce enemies against whom they had to protect themselves. I mean, it was deeply imbued in the general culture—in part including German Jews. There's a book by a major humanistic figure of modern Jewish life, Joachim Prinz. He was in Germany in the '30s, and he wrote a book called *Wir Juden* (We Jews), in which he said, Look, we don't like the anti-Semitic undertones of what the Nazis are doing, but we should bear in mind that much of what they're saying is right, and we agree with it. In particular their emphasis on blood and land—*Blut und Boden*. Basically we agree with that. We think that the identity of blood is very important, and the emphasis on the land is very important. And the tie between blood and land is important. And in fact as late as 1941, influential figures in the Jewish Palestinian community, the pre-state community, including the group headed by Yitzhak Shamir, who later became Prime Minister, and leading intellectuals, considered rather left intellectuals, sent a delegation to try to reach, I think, Himmler—somebody high up—to tell them that they would like to make an arrangement with the Germans, and they would be the outpost for Germany in the Middle East, because they basically agreed with them on a lot of things. Like these things. This was, I think, in January, 1941. Now, no one would suggest this was the mainstream, by any means, but it also wasn't a pathological fringe.

I mean, George Kennan, who, in the spectrum of policy-makers, is sort of on the humane liberal side, was the American consul in Berlin before the war, before Pearl Harbor. And I think it must have been in mid-April, 1941, pretty late, he was sending back messages saying, you know, we shouldn't be too critical of the Nazis, they were doing some bad things, but there are good things about them, and we have to recognize the importance of what they're doing in holding back the Bolsheviks and suppressing the labor movement and so on. Roosevelt, too. Roosevelt was always quite pro-Fascist, thought Mussolini was "that admirable Italian gentleman," as he called him. As late as 1939, he was saying that Fascism was an important experiment that they were carrying out, until it was distorted by the relation to Hitler. And this was almost twenty years after they destroyed the Parliament, broke up the labor movement, raided Ethiopia with all the atrocities . . .

WS: A lot of people feel that hope for humanity lies not so much in the progress of rationality but rather in the possibility that more people will fall under the influence of moral principles or moral codes, such as the ethical systems developed by various religions. After all, if everyone were seriously committed to moral ideals, then . . .

NC: Moral codes . . . You can find things in the traditional religions which are very benign and decent and wonderful and so on, but I mean, the Bible is probably the most genocidal book in the literary canon. The God of the Bible—not only did he order His chosen people to carry out literal genocide—I mean, wipe out every Amalekite to the last man, woman, child, and, you know, donkey and so on, because hundreds of years ago they got in your way when you were trying to cross the desert—not only did He do things like that, but, after all, the God of the Bible was ready to destroy every living creature on earth because some humans irritated Him. That's the story of Noah. I mean, that's *beyond* genocide—you don't know how to describe this creature. Somebody offended Him, and He was going to destroy every living being on earth? And then He was talked into allowing two of each species to stay alive—that's supposed to be gentle and wonderful.

WS: Hmm . . . If moral codes themselves can't be relied upon, it's hard to know what to cling to if we want to avoid falling into moral nightmares. In a way, it seems to be simply our obsessive need to have a high opinion of ourselves that leads us repeatedly into idiotic thinking. If our vestigial rationality detects a conflict between our actions and our principles—well, we don't want to change our actions, and it's embarrassing to change our principles, so we wield the blow-torch against our rationality, bending it till it's willing to say that our principles and actions are well-aligned. We're prisoners of self-love.

NC: We understand the crimes of others but can't understand our own. Take that picture over there on the wall. What it is is the Angel of Death, obviously. Off on the right is Archbishop Romero, who was assassinated in 1980. The figures below are the six leading Jesuit intellectuals who had their brains blown out in 1989, and their housekeeper and her daughter, who were also murdered. Now, they were murdered by an elite battalion armed, trained, and directed by the United States. The Archbishop was murdered pretty much by the same hands. Well, a couple of weeks ago there was a court case in California where some members of the family of Romero brought some kind of a civil suit against one of the likely killers and actually won their case. Well, that's a pretty important precedent, but it was barely reported in the United States. Nobody wants to listen. You know, Czeslaw Milosz was a courageous, good person. And when he died there were huge stories. But he and his associates faced nothing in Eastern Europe like what intellectuals faced in our domains. I mean, Havel was put in jail. He didn't have his brains blown out by elite battalions trained by the Russians. In Rwanda, for about a hundred days they were killing about eight thousand people a day. And we just went through the tenth anniversary. There was a lot of lamentation about how we didn't do anything about it, and how awful, and we ought to do something about other people's crimes, and so on. That's an easy one—to do something about other people's crimes. But you know, every single day, about the same number of people—children—are dying in Southern Africa from easily treatable diseases. Are we doing anything about it? I mean, that's Rwanda-level killing, just children, just Southern Africa, every day—not a hundred days but all the time. It doesn't take military intervention. We don't need to worry about who's going to protect our forces. What it takes is bribing totalitarian institutions to produce drugs. It costs pennies. Do we think about it? Do we do it? Do we ask what kind of a civilization is it where we have to bribe totalitarian institutions in order to get them to produce drugs to stop Rwanda-level killing every day? It's just easier not to think about it.

WS: Totalitarian institutions—you mean the drug companies?

NC: Yes. What are they? The drug companies are just totalitarian institutions which are subsidized: most of the basic research is funded by the public, there are huge profits, and of course from a business point of view it not only makes sense, but it's legally required for them to produce lifestyle drugs for rich Westerners to get rid of wrinkles, instead of malaria treatments for dying children in Africa. It's required. It's legally required.

WS: How do we get out from under that?

NC: Well, the first thing we have to do is face it. Until you face it, you can't get out from under it. Take fairly recent things like the feminist movement—women's rights. I mean, if you had asked my grandmother if she was oppressed she would have said no. She wouldn't have known what you were talking about. Of course she was stuck in the kitchen all day, and she followed orders. And the idea that her husband would do anything around the house . . . I mean, my mother would not *allow* my father, or me, for that matter, into the kitchen. Literally. Because we were supposed to be studying the Talmud or something. But did they think they were oppressed? Well, actually, my mother already felt that she was. But my grandmother didn't. And to get that awareness—you know, it's not easy.

India is interesting in this respect. There have been some very careful studies, and one of the best was about the province of Uttar Pradesh. It has one of the lowest female to male ratios in the world, not because of female infanticide, but because of the shitty way women are treated. And I mean, I was shocked to discover that in the town where I live, Lexington, which is a professional, upper middle class community—you know, doctors, lawyers, academics, stockbrokers, mostly that sort of thing—the police have a special unit for domestic abuse which has two or three 911 calls a week. Now, you know, that's important. Because thirty years ago, they *didn't* have that, because domestic abuse was not considered a problem. Now at least it's considered a problem, and police forces deal with it, and the courts deal with it in some fashion. Well, you know, that takes work—it takes work to recognize that oppression is going on.

This was very striking to me in the student movement in the '60s. I mean, I was pretty close to it, and those kids were involved in something very serious. You know, they were very upset, and they hated the war, and they hated racism, and their choices weren't always the right ones by any means, but they were very emotional about it, for very good reasons. . . .

I was involved particularly with the resisters, who were refusing to serve in the army. They're now called "draft evaders" and so on, but that's bullshit. I mean, almost all of them could have gotten out of the draft easily. A lot of them were theology students, and others—you'd go to your doctor, and he'd say you were a homosexual or something. It was nothing for a privileged kid to get out of the army if he wanted to. They were *choosing* to resist. And facing serious penalties. For an eighteen-year-old kid to go to jail for years or live their life in exile was not an easy choice—especially when, of course, if you conformed, you would just shoot up there and be part of the elite. But they chose it, and it was a courageous decision, and they were denounced for it and condemned for it and so on. . . . At some stage of the game, the feminist movement began. In the early stages of the resistance, the women were supposed to be supportive, you know, to these resisters. And at some stage these young women began to ask, Why are we doing the shit-work? I mean, why are we the ones who are supposed to look up in awe at *them*, when we're doing most of the work? And they began to regard themselves as being oppressed. Now that caused a rather serious psychological problem for the boys. Because they thought, and rightly, that they were doing something courageous and noble, and here suddenly they had to face up to the fact that they were oppressors, and that was hard. I mean, I know people who committed suicide. Literally. Because they couldn't face it.

So, just in our lifetime, it's different. The kinds of things that were considered normal—not just normal, un-noticeable, you didn't see them—thirty or forty years ago, would be unspeakable now. The same with gay rights. There have been big changes in consciousness, and they're important, and they make it a better world. But they do not affect *class* issues. Class is a dirty word in the United States. You can't talk about it.

One of my daughters teaches in a state college in which the aspirations of most of the students are to become a nurse or a policeman. The first day of class (she teaches history) she usually asks her students to identify their class background. And it turns out there are two answers. Either they're middle class, or they're underclass. If their father has a job, like as a janitor, they're middle class. If their father is in jail or transient, then it's underclass. That's it. Nobody's working class. It's just not a concept that exists. It's not just here—it's true in England too. I was in England a couple of months ago at the time of the Cannes Festival, when Michael Moore won, and one of the papers had a long interview with him, and the interviewer was suggesting that Michael Moore wasn't telling the truth when he said he came from a working class background. He said he came from a working class background, but his father had a car and owned a house, so, you know, what's this crap about coming from a working class background? Well, his father was an auto worker! I mean, the whole concept of class in any meaningful sense has just been driven out of people's heads. The fact that there are some people who give the orders and others who follow them—that is gone. And the only question is, how many goods do you have?— as if, if you have goods, you have to be middle class, even if you're just following the orders.

WS: What you possess determines how people see you and

how you see yourself. That defines you—your role in the social structure does not.

NC: People are trained—and massive efforts go into this—people are trained to perceive their identity and their aspirations and their value as people in terms of the things they amass. Nothing else. And in terms of *yourself*, not anyone else . . . It's kind of interesting to watch this campaign against Social Security going on, and to see the attitudes. I see it even among students. And the reason certain people hate Social Security so much is not just that if you privatize it, it's a bonanza for Wall Street. I'm sure that's part of it, but the main reason for the real visceral hatred of Social Security is that it's based on a principle that they want to drive out of people's heads—namely, that you care about somebody else. You know, Social Security is based on the idea that you care whether the disabled widow on the other side of town has enough food to eat. And you're not supposed to think that. That's a dangerous sentiment. You're supposed to just be out for yourself. And I get this from young people now. They say, Look, I don't see why I should be responsible for her. I'm not responsible for her. I didn't do anything to her. I mean, if she didn't invest properly or, you know, something like that, that's not my business. Why do I have to pay my taxes to keep her alive? And why do I care if the kid down the street can't go to school? I mean, *I* didn't keep him from going to school.

WS: But isn't that sort of demonstrably absurd? I mean, the student who doesn't think he's involved with the other people is simply wrong. He is not a self-created atom. He's a part of society and was created by society. He didn't become whatever he is simply through his own individual efforts. It was society that gave him everything he has and everything he's ever used. He didn't invent the English language. He didn't invent the telephone.

NC: Yes, but people are very deluded about this, including professionals. Take professional economists. Most of them literally believe what Alan Greenspan and others talk about—that the economy flourishes because of entrepreneurial initiative and consumer choice and so on and so forth. You know, that's total bullshit. The economy flourishes because we have a dynamic state sector.

WS: You mean, the motor driving it all is the taxpayer's money being spent—or given away to private companies—by the state. The motor is *not* the individual consumer spending his money in the free market.

NC: Just about everything in the new economy comes out of state initiatives. I mean, what's M.I.T.? M.I.T. is overwhelmingly a taxpayer-funded institution, in which research and development is carried out at public cost and risk, and if anything comes out of it, some private corporation, like the guys who endowed this building, will get the profit from it. And almost everything works like that—from computers, internet, telecommunications, pharmaceuticals—you run through the dynamic parts of the economy, that's where they come from. I mean, with things like, say, computers and the internet, for example, consumer choice had no role at all! Consumers didn't even know these things existed until they'd been developed for years at public expense. But we live in a world of illusion.

WS: People's view of how it's all working is wrong. And of course most people are just totally immersed intellectually in their own personal economic struggle — their struggle to get, basically, things. But you know, when you say that people are trained to focus their aspirations entirely on things — goods — well, that has terrifying implications. To say that people may not even be aware that their lives consist of following orders — that's terrifying. It's as if people don't acknowledge that their ability to make choices about their lives, their degree of power over their own environment, is an important issue.

NC: No, what you're taught from infancy is that the only choices you're supposed to make are choices of commodities. It's none of your business how the government works or what government policies are or how the community's organized or anything else. Your job is to purchase commodities. And that's been put in people's heads from infancy. And that's why we have farcical elections. I mean, the elections do not turn on issues. I mean, nobody knows where the candidates stand on issues. It would take a research project to figure out where they stand on health care or something — if they even have a position. I mean, what you're supposed to focus on are qualities. You know, Is he a "strong leader"? Is he going to protect us? Is he likeable? Would you like to meet him in a bar? I mean, the thing that's called an election here — we would simply ridicule it if it were happening somewhere else. I mean, what's the election? — you know, two guys—same background—wealth, political influence, went to the same elite university, joined the same secret society where you're trained to be a ruler—they both can run because they're financed by the same corporate institutions. At the Democratic Convention, Barack Obama said, "Only in this country, only in America, could someone like me appear here." Well, in some other countries, people much poorer than him would not only talk at the convention—they'd be elected president! Take Lula. The president of Brazil is a guy with a peasant background, a union organizer, never went to school, he's the president of the second-biggest country in the hemisphere! Only in America? I mean, there they actually have elections where you can choose somebody from your own ranks. With different policies! That's inconceivable in the United States. And it's true of even the dissidents. There is a huge propaganda effort to reduce political participation to showing up every four years to push a lever in a personalized electoral extravaganza, and then go home and let "your representatives" run the world. Dissidents are often caught up in this too, and reinforce these delusions. Presidential elections exist, and can't be ignored. But the real world of serious political action isn't a once-in-four-years vote-for-me affair. That's not the way Lula got elected.

A lot of it's conscious. There's a conscious strain in sort of liberal, intellectual thought, it goes way back, that the people really don't have any right to participate in the political system. They are supposed to choose among the responsible men.

WS: But it's funny that the people themselves go along with it, because it seems insulting. Why aren't people more insulted?

They're not even insulted when they're blatantly lied to! They seem to laugh it off. But in their own lives, in daily life, people would resent it a lot—you know, being lied to.

NC: No—not when people in power lie to you. Somehow there's some law that that's the way it works. I mean, do people get upset if their boss lies to them?

WS: Maybe not, maybe not . . . Well, you know, what you've been saying is scary, but it's also invigorating in a way. Obviously you're not a particularly sentimental person, I would say, and it's not your style to make starry-eyed statements, but in a way you're opening up a rather extraordinary vision of human possibility here. I feel like saying that your approach to discussing these things is a bit like the approach of a sculptor—with hammer and chisel you attack the big block of marble, and from a certain point of view, all your gestures could be seen as rather hostile or aggressive as you pursue the somewhat negative activity of cutting down the stone, but in the end something rather glorious is revealed. You're suggesting that rather than being deluded and passive intellectual followers of the prevailing world-view of our time and place, we might wake up and think for ourselves. And I think you're suggesting that all human beings have the capacity to collaborate in the task of guiding their own lives, and the life of the place where they work, and the life of their community, and the life of the world. And that to live in illusion, to be a slave to the world-view of your time and place, or to be all your life a follower of orders, or to not even be aware that you have the capacity to participate in the direction of things—these are all in a way different forms of oppression. And it's a terrible thing, but people go along with it.

NC: Slaves went along with it, women went along with it, oppressed people often go along with it. Until they—I mean, to learn that you *are* being oppressed, and you don't have to be, is hard.

WS: Right. It's hard. That's an understatement. But it's something to work for, over the centuries, if we survive. Anyway—thanks. For the interview and in general.

The Webern Variations

by Mark Strand

The sudden rush of it
pushing aside the branches,
late summer flashing towards
the image of its absence

*

Into the heart of nothing,
into the radiant hollows,
even the language of vanishing
leaves itself behind

*

Clouds, trees, houses,
in the feeling they awaken
as the dark approaches, seem
like pieces of another life

*

One can sift through what remains—
the dust of phrases uttered once,
the ruins of a passion—
it comes to less each time

*

The voice sliding down,
the voice turning around
and lengthening the thread
of sense, the thread of sound

*

Those avenues of light
that slid between the clouds
moments ago are gone,
and suddenly it is dark

*

Who will be left to stitch
and sew the shroud of song,
the houses back in place, the trees
rising from a purple shade

*

Not too late to see oneself
walk the beach at night,
how easily the sea comes in,
spreads, retreats, and disappears

*

How easily it breathes,
and the late-risen half-moon,
drawn out of darkness, staring down,
seems to pause above the trees

*

Under the moon and stars,
which are what they have always been,
what should we be but ourselves
in this light, which is no light to speak of?

*

What should we hear but the voice
that would be ours shaping itself,
the secret voice of being telling us
that where we disappear is where we are?

*

What to make of a season's end,
the drift of cold drawn down
the hallways of the night,
the wind pushing aside the leaves?

*

The vision of one's passing passes,
days flow into other days,
the voice that sews and stitches
picks up its work once more

*

And everything turns and turns
and the unknown turns into the song
that is the known, but what in turn
becomes of the song is not for us to say

Before the Election—
Fragments from a Diary 2004

by Wallace Shawn

EARLY SEPTEMBER

It's tragic when civilians die in war. But is it really less tragic when soldiers die? Why do people tally the deaths of Iraqi and Afghan civilians—but leave Iraqi and Afghan soldiers out of the accounting? Did the soldiers in those miserable armies deserve to die? Because they were soldiers? These were just young men—some were conscripted against their will, others decided to risk their lives and enlist (maybe because they were desperate, because they were ignorant, because they loved their country). Please don't tell me they deserved to be massacred and not even counted.

Who does deserve to die? Whose death should not be mourned? Many would answer: the guilty deserve to die and should not be mourned.

A farmer wakes up in the morning and says, "I hope I can plant the seeds today before it starts to rain." An artist wakes up in the morning and says, "I hope I paint something worthwhile today." But those who control arsenals of weapons wake up quite differently. Bush wakes up in the morning, looks at himself in the mirror, and says, "I'll kill people today." Bin Laden wakes up and says, "I'll kill people today." They believe they're gods, appropriately wielding power over life and death. They believe that the ones they will kill are guilty of crimes and deserve to die.

To Bush, an Afghan who fought for the Taliban is guilty of a crime, because he helped to support the government of his country, which helped a man who killed Americans. To bin Laden, a secretary at the World Trade Center is guilty of a crime, because she worked for a corporation which was one of the building-blocks of the world structure which kills Arabs.

Of course there are particular instances in which even hardened killers find it too absurd to claim that that their chosen victims are guilty of crimes and deserve their deaths. This is particularly the case when the victims are children. In those cases—the Chechen rebels' seizure of child hostages, Clinton's use of child-killing sanctions in Iraq—the claim is simply that the absolute necessity of achieving the goal (the liberation from Russian oppression, the hostile leverage applied to Saddam Hussein's regime) allows the killing of the innocent to become appropriate.

A lot of hypocrisy comes into play in discussions about killing.

I myself found the Sandinista Revolution a wonderful thing, although it was led by people who took it upon themselves to kill in order to achieve their purpose. I rejoiced at the end of apartheid, although it wouldn't have ended if it hadn't been for the activities of the A.N.C., which took it upon itself to kill in order to end apartheid. When you live in a place where oppression is murdering your countrymen every day, where people are cold and have no blankets or shelter, where people are hungry, where people are starving, where people's lives are being crushed by the status quo, you may feel a desperate need to take immediate action, and the human imagination is only rarely capable of devising and embracing a Gandhian approach to the necessary confrontation with the ruling powers. So at times a simple choice appears to exist between the human death daily caused by the existing system and the use of force to effect change. And to denounce all of those whose battle for change has not excluded violent methods may be to condemn most people on earth to inevitable suffocation. There may always be a third, non-violent path, but it's the hardest to see. Yes, if I'm involved, I must struggle to find it, but I can't bring myself to condemn Mandela and everyone else whose principled struggle for justice fell short of the non-violent ideal.

Nonetheless, I always come back to the feeling that it's basically horrifying for an individual to decide about himself, "Yes, my cause is just, and so I grant myself the power over life and death, I grant myself the right to kill, I grant myself the right to kill the guilty, I grant myself the right to kill the innocent."

The most hypocritical on the subject of killing are the gigantic killers. And the consequences of this at the present moment are desperately frightening. Bush said at the Republican Convention, " I will never relent in defending America—whatever it takes." And the most dangerous aspect of his infinitely dangerous phrase "war on terror" is the reduction of the enemy to a non-human abstraction, as if Osama bin Laden and all Muslims who violently oppose the actions of the United States are so profoundly immoral and alien that they cannot even be confronted as human beings but can only be seen as a swarm of creatures to be exterminated—creatures whom one cannot imagine even understanding human speech, creatures with whom no exchange or communication is even remotely possible.

To call this attitude hypocrisy is simply to say: Yes, it *is* hard to believe that any human beings could be so inhuman as to crash planes into the World Trade Center, but it also happens to be hard to believe that any human beings could massacre the defenseless Zulus, entire families, as the British did in the days of the Empire, or rape and murder occupied populations, as the Japanese did in World War II, or systematically, relentlessly drop explosives and napalm from gleaming airplanes onto peasant village after peasant village, year after year, as the Americans did in the Vietnam War. The Americans happen to have destroyed the city of Hiroshima with an atomic bomb, so it's living in a fantasy world for Americans to pretend to be shocked by the vileness of bin Laden. Bin Laden and his followers have a point of view for which they're willing to kill — in other words, they're like the others, they're like us. Some of what bin Laden thinks is quite reasonable. Like Paul Wolfowitz, like Pat Robertson, like Ariel Sharon, like George Bush, bin Laden thinks a lot of things which are *not* reasonable. Is bin Laden crazy? Maybe he is, I really don't know. Are all of the people who admire him throughout the Arab world crazy? I really don't think so. It matters quite a lot, because if they're not crazy, they would eventually understand it if we showed some respect for their lives and their concerns. If we started to listen, they'd eventually realize that we were in fact listening.

LATE SEPTEMBER — AUTUMN BEGINS

Not unlike those unfortunate individuals who have somehow become addicted to pornography on the internet, a frightening number of Americans seek relief in nationalistic fantasy from the unsatisfying incompleteness of their daily lives — and then become hooked. It's been going on for years. Their particular dream is not about sex or pleasure, it's not even about beautiful fields or ocean waves — instead it's about blood which is flowing from the wounds of the enemies of the nation. And just as the male heterosexual pornography addict identifies with, and revels in the exploits of, the triumphant naked male in the pornographic scene, the nationalism addict identifies with the soldier, the bomber, and above all the president. The end of the Cold War was a moment of anxiety for the American nationalism addict. Pornography privileges were suddenly removed. The apparently implacable Soviet leaders, sitting perennially in a row behind those stiff-looking tables, disappeared from the television screens, along with the trudging, ill-clad armies of "Marxist guerrillas" in various countries around the world, and so, just as ex-alcoholics (like President Bush) are nonplussed, or worse, by the sudden disappearance of their necessary substance, nationalism addicts in the 1990s experienced serious depression if not desperation. But in 2001, the emergence of "the terrorists" finally brought relief. In fact, "the terrorists" were an improvement, as the Russians had never actually attacked the United States, nor had their statements expressed visceral loathing against us.

One of the peculiarities of heterosexual pornography made for men is that so much screen-time is given to the penis, and one of the peculiarities of nationalistic fantasy is that so much of the dream is about the wonderfulness of the national self as the blows are being struck, while little curiosity is directed actually to the characteristics of the bleeding victim/enemy. The mental camera focuses on the noble intentions and plans of the slaughterer, while the supposedly once-dangerous victim offers up blood and cries but apparently possesses no intentions, thoughts, or feelings at all.

The eighteenth century figures who devised the theory of modern democracy, not to mention the Ancient Greeks, had something else in mind. Perhaps it's naïve of me to think this, but I believe they imagined that citizens would live and vote based on a rational consideration of their own interests and convictions. I think they believed that a political speech was intended to convince its audience

35

of a point of view—to persuade them through a rational marshalling of evidence and inferences. To put a drug into someone's drink, knock them out, and carry them home is not a form of seduction, and paralyzing a person's brain with fantasy—whether injected by a needle through the skull or poured into the ears through the spoken word—is not a form of rational argument, nor any basis for what those theorists would have called "democracy."

On almost every subject of serious importance, but most particularly in regard to what life in other countries is actually like, and what the effects of American policy in regard to those other countries actually might be, the American citizen is drowning in a sort of honey of lies, and the truth, for most people, is absolutely unavailable. Fantasies are available, and dreams are available, but the truth is not available. The American citizen's vote for a particular candidate may well result in anguish and destruction for thousands of people in some distant land on the other side of the world, but the citizen who cast the vote has no idea that this could possibly be the case.

If Politician A plans to raise taxes but promises to lower them, and Politician B plans to lower taxes but promises to raise them, a citizen may vote in a voting booth, but he is voting in such ignorance that it becomes ridiculous to call his vote an example of "democracy." Still less is it "democracy" if he wanders into the booth in a hallucinated daze, casting his vote, as he believes, for the candidate representing elves rather than for the candidate representing satyrs, because he believes that the elves will give him candy but that the satyrs are ugly and may want to eat him.

"Democracy" is meaningless—voting is meaningless—if the citizens who vote do not know the meaning of their own vote.

Yes, the citizens hold a great power in their hands. Yes, the citizen's vote will have consequences. But if the citizen has no idea what those consequences might be, one can only find his power alarming. One can hardly admire the fact that he has it. It's poignant to think how much we admired our political system when we were growing up, how much everyone we knew admired it, because of the power of the citizen. But our pride was based on an idea that the citizen knew what was going on.

To tell pleasing falsehoods to a blind man or woman in a dangerous environment is ultimately not helpful or particularly nice, and you might say that this is what the newspapers, the television networks, and the politicians, for their different reasons, have been doing to all of us. The newspapers and the networks are commercial enterprises whose goal is basically to win large audiences by amusing them and pleasing them. The politicians also are trying to please—they hope to win elections by telling the public a flattering story about itself. Neither the commercial journalist nor the political candidate ultimately wants to alienate the potentially defensive and self-protective listeners by suddenly revealing that their treasured myths are based on lies, even though in the long run this knowledge might be absolutely necessary to the listeners' survival. The long-term welfare of the audience is not the entertainer's concern.

A collection of drugged, semi-conscious individuals are simply prey for whoever is drugging them—they can't constitute a democratic community. If most of what they hear is a lie, and most of what they know is a lie, they are obviously not in a position to make rational choices. And Americans who do not go to libraries to seek out independent accounts of historical events, and who hear repeatedly from the Republican candidate (who believes it) and from the Democratic candidate (who is consciously lying) that the Vietnam War was an honorable struggle by the United States, cannot think rationally about the Vietnam War or the character of their own nation. And if people have heard from the Democratic candidate and from the Republican candidate and from everyone they listen to and everyone they know that "the terrorists" attacked the United States in 2001 because they are "filled with hate" for no reason at all, then they cannot think rationally about the things that are happening in the world, and they cannot be said to be participating in something called "democracy" in any sense intended by the eighteenth century thinkers.

The Democrats join the Republicans in feeding people lies, and in nourishing their addiction to fantasy, despite the fact that individual Democrats may hope to return to the path of truth once the expedient deceits have paved the way to their political success. But that's a dangerous game. Every lie that you convincingly tell increases the confidence of the one who believes it that his current view of life is indeed correct, and so it's going to be that much harder, at some time in the future, to persuade that person that his view is wrong. And if circumstances change, and the liar would like to take back his lie, he's unable to do so without running the risk that everyone will know he was lying earlier. Lies ruin the one who believes them, taking him out of reality, and they ruin the teller, because he becomes constrained to act as if what he once knew to be true had somehow become false.

Twilight of the Superheroes

by Deborah Eisenberg

NATHANIEL RECALLS THE MIRACLE

The grandchildren approach.

Nathaniel can make them out dimly in the shadows. When it's time, he'll tell them about the miracle.

It was the dawn of the New Millennium, he'll say. *I was living in the Midwest back then, but my friends from college persuaded me to come to New York.*

I arrived a few days ahead of the amazing occasion, and all over the city there was an atmosphere of feverish anticipation. The Year Two Thousand! The New Millennium! Some people thought it was sure to be the end of the world. Others thought we were at the threshold of something completely new, and better. The tabloids carried wild predictions from celebrity clairvoyants, and even people who scoffed and said that the date was an arbitrary and meaningless one were secretly agitated. In short, we were suddenly aware of ourselves standing there, staring at the future blindfolded.

I suppose, looking back on it, that all the commotion seems comical and ridiculous. And perhaps you're thinking that we churned it up to entertain ourselves because we were bored or because our lives felt too easy—trivial and mundane. But consider: ceremonial occasions, even purely personal ones like birthdays or anniversaries, remind us that the world is full of terrifying surprises and no one knows what even the very next second will bring!

Well, shortly before the momentous day, a strange news item appeared: experts were saying that a little mistake had been made— just one tiny mistake, a little detail in the way computers everywhere had been programmed. But the consequences of this detail, the experts said, were potentially disastrous; tiny as it was, the detail might affect everybody, and in a very big way!

You see, if history has anything to teach us, it's that (despite all our efforts, despite our best—or worst—intentions, despite the touchingly indestructible faith we have in our own foresight) we poor humans cannot actually think ahead; there are just too many variables. And when it comes down to it, it always turns out that no one is in charge of the things that really matter.

It must be hard for you to imagine—it's even hard for me to remember—but people hadn't been using computers for very long. As far as I know, my mother (your great grandmother) never even touched one! And no one had thought to inform the computers that one day the universe would pass from the years of the one thousands into the years of the two thousands. So the machines, as these experts had suddenly realized, were not equipped to understand that at the conclusion of 1999 time would not start over from 1900, time would keep going.

People all over America—all over the world!—began to speak of "a crisis of major proportions," (which was a phrase we used to use back then). Because, all the routine operations that we'd so blithely delegated to computers, the operations we all took for granted and depended on—how would they proceed?

Might one be fatally trapped in an elevator? Would we have to huddle together for warmth and scrabble frantically through our pockets for a pack of fancy restaurant matches so we could set our stacks of old New York Reviews ablaze? Would all the food that was supposed to be trucked from countryside to city rot in heaps out there on the highways, leaving us to pounce on fat old street rats and grill them over the flames? What was going to happen to our bank accounts—would they vaporize? And what about air traffic control? On December 31st when the second hand moved from 11:59:59 to midnight, would all the airplanes in the sky collide?

Everyone was thinking of more and more alarming possibilities. Some people committed their last night on this earth to partying, and others rushed around buying freeze-dried provisions and cases of water and flashlights and radios and heavy blankets, in the event that the disastrous problem might somehow eventually be solved.

And then, as the clock ticked its way through the enormous gatherings in celebration of the era that was due to begin in a matter of hours, then minutes, then seconds, we waited to learn the terrible consequences of the tiny oversight. Khartoum, Budapest, Paris—we watched on television, our hearts fluttering, as midnight, first just a tiny speck in the East, unfurled gently, darkening the sky and moving toward us over the globe.

But the amazing thing—Nathaniel will tell his grandchildren—*was that nothing happened! We held our breath . . . And there was nothing! It was a miracle. Over the face of the earth, from east to west and back again, nothing catastrophic happened at all.*

Oh, well. Frankly, by the time he or any of his friends get around to producing a grandchild (or even a child, come to think of it) they might well have to explain what computers had been. And freeze-dried provisions. And celebrity clairvoyants and airplanes and New York and America and even cities, and heaven only knows what.

FROGBOIL

Lucien watches absently as his assistant, Sharmila, prepares to close up the gallery for the evening; something keeps tugging at his attention . . .

Oh, yes. It's the phrase Yoshi Matsumoto had used this morning when he called from Tokyo. *Back to normal . . . Back to normal . . .*

What's that famous, revolting, sadistic experiment? Something like, you drop the frog into a pot of boiling water and it jumps out. But if you drop it into a pot of cold water and slowly bring the water to a boil, the frog stays put and gets boiled.

Itami Systems is reopening their New York branch, was what Matsumoto called to tell Lucien; he'll be returning to the city soon. Lucien pictured his old friend's mournful, ironic expression as he added "They tell me they're 'exploring additional avenues of development now that New York is back to normal.'"

Lucien had made an inadvertent squawklike sound. He shook his head, then he shook his head again.

"Hello?" Matsumoto said.

"I'm here," Lucien said. "Well, it'll be good to see you again. But steel yourself for a wait at customs; they're fingerprinting."

VIEW

Mr. Matsumoto's loft is a jungle of big rubbery trees, under which crouch sleek items of chrome and leather. Spindly electronic devices blink or warble amid the foliage, and here and there one comes upon an immense flat-screen TV—the first of their kind that Nathaniel ever handled.

Nathaniel and his friends have been subletting—thanks, obviously, to Uncle Lucien—for a ridiculously minimal rent and on Mr. Matsumoto's highly tolerable conditions of cat sitting and general upkeep. Nathaniel and Lyle and Amity and Madison each have something like an actual bedroom, and there are three whole bathrooms, one equipped with a Jacuzzi. The kitchen, stone and steel, has cupboards bigger than most of their friends' apartments. Art— important, soon to be important, or very recently important—most of which was acquired from Uncle Lucien—hangs on the walls.

And the terrace! One has only to open the magic sliding panel to find oneself halfway to heaven. On the evening, over three years ago, when Uncle Lucien completed the arrangements for Nathaniel to sublet and showed him the place, Nathaniel stepped out onto the terrace and tears shot right up into his eyes.

There was that unearthly palace, The Chrysler Building! There was The Empire State Building, like a brilliant violet hologram! There were the vast, twinkling prairies of Brooklyn and New Jersey! And best of all, Nathaniel could make out the Statue of Liberty holding her torch aloft, as she had held it for each of his parents when they arrived as children from across the ocean, terrified, filthy, and hungry, to safety.

Stars glimmered nearby; towers and spires, glowing emerald, topaz, ruby, sapphire, soared below. The avenues and bridges slung a trembling net of light across the rivers, over the buildings. Everything was spangled and dancing; the little boats glittered. The lights floated up and up like bubbles.

Back when Nathaniel moved into Mr. Matsumoto's loft, shortly after his millennial arrival in New York, sitting out on the terrace had been like looking down over the rim into a gigantic glass of champagne.

UNCLE LUCIEN'S WORDS OF REASSURANCE

So, Matsumoto is returning. And Lucien has called Nathaniel, the nephew of his adored late wife, Charlie, to break the news.

Well, of course it's hardly a catastrophe for the boy. Matsumoto's place was only a sublet in any case, and Nathaniel and his friends will all find other apartments.

But it's such an ordeal in this city. And all four of the young people, however different they might be, strike Lucien as being in some kind of holding pattern—as if they're temporizing, or muffled by unspoken reservations. Of course, he doesn't really know them. Maybe it's just the eternal, poignant weariness of youth.

The strangest thing about getting old (or one of the many strangest things) is that young people sometimes appear to Lucien—as, in fact, Sharmila does at this very moment—in a nimbus of tender light. It's as if her unrealized future were projecting outward like ectoplasm.

"Doing anything entertaining this evening?" he asks her.

She sighs. "Time will tell," she says.

She's a nice young woman; he'd like to give her a few words of advice, or reassurance.

But what could they possibly be? "Don't—" he begins.

Don't worry? HAHAHAHAHA! Don't feel *sad*? "Don't bother about the phones," is what he settles down on. A new show goes up tomorrow, and it's become Lucien's custom on such evenings to linger in the stripped gallery and have a glass of wine. "I'll take care of them later."

But how has he *gotten* so old?

SUSPENSION

So, there was the famous, strangely blank New Year's Eve, the nothing at all that happened, neither the apocalypse nor the failure of the planet's computers, nor, evidently, the dawning of a better age. Nathaniel went to parties with his old friends from school and was asleep before dawn; the next afternoon he awoke with only a mild hangover and an uneasy impression of something left undone.

Next thing you knew, along came that slump, as it was called— the general economic blight that withered the New York branch of Mr. Matsumoto's firm and clusters of jobs all over the city. There appeared to be no jobs at all, in fact, but, amazingly, Uncle Lucien unearthed one for Nathaniel in the architectural division of the subway system. It was virtually impossible to afford an apartment, but Uncle Lucien arranged, also amazingly, for Nathaniel to sublet Mr. Matsumoto's loft.

Then Madison and his girlfriend broke up, so Madison moved into Mr. Matsumoto's, too. Not long afterwards, the brokerage house where Amity was working collapsed (resoundingly) and she'd joined them. Then Lyle's landlord jacked up his rent, so Lyle started living at Mr. Matsumoto's as well.

And as the return of Mr. Matsumoto to New York was contingent upon the return of a reasonable business climate, one way or another it had sort of slipped their minds that Mr. Matsumoto was real. And for over three years there they've been, hanging in temporary luxury 31 floors above the pavement.

They're all out on the terrace this evening. Madison has brought in champagne so that they can salute with an adequate flourish the end of their tenure in Mr. Matsumoto's place. And except for Amity, who takes a principled stand against thoughtful moods, and Amity's new friend or possibly suitor, Russell, who has no history here, they're kind of quiet.

REUNION

Now that Sharmila has gone, Lucien's stunning, cutting edge gallery space blurs a bit and recedes. The room, in fact, seems almost like an old snapshot from that bizarre, quaintly futuristic century, the twentieth. Lucien takes a bottle of white wine from the little fridge in the office, pours himself a glass, and from behind a door in that century, emerges Charlie.

Charlie—Oh, how long it's been, how unbearably long! Lucien luxuriates in the little pulse of warmth just under his skin that indicates her presence. He strains for traces of her voice, but her words degrade like the words in a dream, as if they're being rubbed through a sieve.

Yes, yes, Lucien assures her. He'll put his mind to finding another apartment for her nephew. And when her poor, exasperating sister and brother-in-law call frantically about Nathaniel, as they're bound to do, he'll do his best to calm them down.

But what a nuisance it all is! The boy is as opaque to his parents as a turnip. He was the child of their old age and he's also, obviously, the repository of all of their baroque hopes and fears. By their own account, they throw up their hands and wring them, lecture Nathaniel about frugality then press spending money upon him and fret when he doesn't use it.

Between Charlie's death and Nathaniel's arrival in New York, Lucien heard from Rose and Isaac only at what they considered moments of emergency: Nathaniel's grades were erratic! His friends were peculiar! Nathaniel had expressed an interest in architecture, an unreliable future! He drew, and Lucien had better sit down, *comics*!

The lamentations would pour through the phone, and then, the instant Lucien hung up, evaporate. But if he had given the matter one moment's thought, he realizes, he would have understood from very early on that it was only a matter of time until the boy found his way to the city.

It was about four years ago now that Rose and Isaac put in an especially urgent call. Lucien held the receiver at arm's length and gritted his teeth. "You're an important man," Rose was shouting. "We understand that, we understand how busy you are, you know we'd never call, but it's an emergency. The boy's in New York, and he sounds terrible. He doesn't have a job, lord only knows what he eats — I don't know what to think, Lucien, he *drifts*, he's just *drifting*. Call him, promise me, that's all I'm asking."

"Fine, certainly, good," Lucien said, already gabbling; he would have agreed to anything if Rose would only hang up.

"But whatever you do," she added, "Please, please, under no circumstances should you let him know that we asked you to call."

Lucien looked at the receiver incredulously. "But how else would I have known he was in New York?" he said. "How else would I have gotten his number?"

There was a silence, and then a brief, amazed laugh from Isaac on another extension. "Well, I don't know what you'll tell him," Isaac said admiringly. "But you're the brains of the family, you'll think of something."

INNOCENCE

And actually, Russell (who seems to be not only Amity's friend and possible suitor but also her agent) has obtained for Amity a whopping big advance from some outfit that Madison refers to as Cheeseball Editions, so whatever else they might all be drinking to (or drinking about) naturally Amity's celebrating a bit. And Russell, recently arrived from LA, cannot suppress his ecstasy about how *ur* New York, as he puts it, Mr. Matsumoto's loft is, tactless as he apparently recognizes this untimely ecstasy to be.

"It's *fantastic*," he says. "Who did it, do you know?"

Nathaniel nods. "Matthias Lehmann."

"That's what I thought, I thought so," Russell says. "It *looks* like

Lehmann. Oh, wow, I can't believe you guys have to move out—I mean, it's just so totally amazing!"

Nathaniel and Madison nod and Lyle sniffs peevishly. Lyle is stretched out on a yoga mat that Nathaniel once bought in preparation for a romance (as yet manqué) with a prettily tattooed yoga teacher he runs into occasionally in the bodega on the corner. Lyle's skin has a waxy, bluish cast; there are dark patches beneath his eyes. He looks like a child too precociously worried to sleep. His boyfriend Jahan has more or less relocated to London, and Lyle has been missing him frantically. Lying there so still on the yoga mat with his eyes closed, he appears to be a tomb sculpture from an as yet non-existent civilization.

"And the view!" Russell says. "This is probably the most incredible view on the *planet*."

The others consider the sight of Russell's eager face. And then Amity says, "More champagne, anyone?"

Well, sure, who knows where Russell had been? Who knows where he would have been on that shining, calm, perfectly blue September morning when the rest of them were here having coffee on the terrace and looked up at the annoying racket of a low flying plane? Why should they expect Russell—now, nearly three years later—to imagine that moment out on the terrace when Lyle spilled his coffee and said oh shit, and something flashed and something tore, and the cloudless sky ignited.

HOME

Rose and Isaac have elbowed their way in behind Charlie, and no matter how forcefully Lucien tries to boot them out, they're making themselves at home, airing their dreary history.

Both sailed as tiny, traumatized children with their separate families and on separate voyages right into the Statue of Liberty's open arms. Rose was almost eleven when her little sister, Charlie, came into being, along with a stainless American birth certificate.

Neither Rose and Charlie's parents nor Isaac's ever recovered from their journey to the New World, to say nothing of what had preceded it. The two sets of old folks spoke, between them, Yiddish, Polish, Russian, German, Croatian, Slovenian, Ukrainian, Rumanian, Latvian, Czech, and Hungarian, Charlie had once told Lucien, but not one of the four ever managed to learn more English than was needed to procure a quarter pound of smoked sturgeon from the deli. They worked impossible hours, they drank a little schnapps, and then, in due course, they died.

Isaac did fairly well manufacturing vacuum cleaners. He and Rose were solid members of their temple and the community, but, according to Charlie, no matter how uneventful their lives in the U.S. continued to be, filling out an unfamiliar form would cause Isaac's hands to sweat and send jets of acid through his innards. When he or Rose encountered someone in uniform—a train conductor, a meter maid, a crossing guard—their hearts would leap into their throats and they would think: *passport*!

Their three elder sons, Nathaniel's brothers, fulfilled Rose and Isaac's deepest hopes by turning out to be blindingly inconspicuous. The boys were so reliable and had so few characteristics it was hard to imagine what anyone could think up to kill them for. They were Jewish, of course, but even Rose and Isaac understood that this particular criterion was inoperative in the U.S.—at least for the time being.

The Old World, danger, and poverty were far in the past. Nevertheless, the family lived in their tidy, Midwestern house with its two-car garage as if secret police were permanently hiding under the matching plastic-covered sofas, as if Brown Shirts and Cossacks were permanently rampaging through the suburban streets.

Lucien knew precious little about vacuum cleaners and nothing at all about childhood infections or lawn fertilizers. And yet, as soon as Charlie introduced him, Isaac and Rose set about soliciting his views as if he were an authority on everything that existed on their shared continent.

His demurrals, disclaimers, and protestations of ignorance were completely ineffective. Whatever guess he was finally strong-armed into hazarding was received as oracular. Oracular!

Fervent gratitude was expressed: Thank God Charlie had brought Lucien into the family! How brilliant he was, how knowledgeable, and how subtle was his understanding of the ways of the world! And then Rose and Isaac would proceed to pick over his poor little opinion as if they were the most ruthless and highly trained lawyers, and on the opposing side.

After Charlie was diagnosed, Lucien had just enough time to understand perfectly what that was to mean. When he was exhausted enough to sleep, he slept as though under heavy anesthetic during an amputation. The pain was not alleviated, but it had been made inscrutable. A frightful thing seemed to lie on top of him, heavy and cold. All night long he would struggle to throw it off, but when dawn delivered him to consciousness, he understood what it was, and that it would never go away.

During his waking hours, the food on his plate would abruptly lose its taste, the painting he was studying would bleach off the canvas, the friend he was talking to would turn into a stranger. And then, one day, he was living in a world all made out of paper, where the sun was a wad of old newspapers and the only sounds were the sounds of tearing paper.

He spoke with Rose and Isaac frequently during Charlie's illness, and they came to New York for her memorial service, where they sat self-consciously and miserably among Lucien and Charlie's attractive friends. He took them to the airport for their return to the Midwest, embraced them warmly, and as they shuffled toward the departure door with the other passengers, turning once to wave, he breathed a sigh of relief: all that, at least, was over, too.

As his senses began to revive, he felt a brief pang—he would miss, in a minor way, the heartrending buffoonery of Charlie's sister and brother-in-law. After all, it had been part of his life with Charlie, even if it had been the only annoying part.

But Charlie's death, instead of setting him utterly, blessedly adrift in his grief, had left him anchored permanently offshore of her family like an island. After a long silence, the infuriating calls started up again. The feudal relationship was apparently inalterable.

CONTEXT

When they'd moved in, it probably *was* the best view on the planet. Then, one morning, out of a clear blue sky, it became, for a while, probably the worst.

For a long time now they've been able to hang out here on the terrace without anyone running inside to be sick or bursting into tears or diving under something at a loud noise or even just making macabre jokes or wondering what sort of debris was settling into their drinks. These days they rarely see—as for a time they invariably did—the sky igniting, the stinking smoke bursting out of it like lava, the tiny figures raining down from the shattered tower as Lyle faints.

But now it's unclear what they are, in fact, looking at—what sort of thing is being engendered in that blank, but far from empty space.

INFORMATION

What would Charlie say about the show that's about to go up? It's work by a youngish Belgian painter who arrived, splashily, on the scene some time after Charlie's departure.

It's good work, but these days Lucien can't get terribly excited about any of the shows. The vibrancy of his brain arranging itself in response to something of someone else's making, the heart's little leap—his gift, reliable for so many years—is gone. Or mostly gone; it's flattened out into something mundane and tepid. It's as if he's got some part that's simply worn out and needs replacing. Let's hope it's still available, he thinks.

How *did* he get so old? The usual stupid question. One had snickered all one's life as the plaintive old geezers doddered about baffled, as if looking for a misplaced sock, tugging one's sleeve, asking sheepishly: *How did I get so old?*

The mere sight of one's patiently blank expression turned them vicious. *It will happen to you*, they'd raged.

Well, all right, it would. But not in the ridiculous way it had happened to *them*. And yet, here he is, he and his friends, falling like so much landfill into the dump of old age. Or at least struggling desperately to balance on the brink. Yet one second ago, running so swiftly toward it, they hadn't even seen it.

And what had happened to his youth? Unlike a misplaced sock, it isn't anywhere; it had dissolved in the making of him.

Surprising that after Charlie's death he did not take the irreversible step. He'd had no appetite to live. But the body has its own appetite, apparently—that pitiless need to continue with its living, which has so many disguises and so many rationales.

A deep embarrassment has been stalking him. Every time he lets his guard down these days, there it is. Because the stark light of calamity has revealed that he and even the most dissolute among his friends simply glided through their lives on the assumption that the sheer fact of their existence made the world in some way a better place. As deranged as it sounds now, a better place. Not a leafy bower, maybe, but still, a somewhat better place—more tolerant, more amenable to the wonderful adventures of the human mind and the human body, more capable of outrage against injustice . . .

For shame! One has been shocked, all one's life, to learn of the blind eye turned to children covered with bruises and welts, the blind eye turned to the men who came at night for the neighbors. And yet . . . And yet one has clung, nonetheless, to the belief that the sun shining inside one's head is evidence of sunshine elsewhere.

Not everywhere, of course. Obviously, at every moment something terrible is being done to someone somewhere—one can't really know about each instance of it!

But frankly—*frankly*—how far away does something have to be before you have the right to not really know about it?

Some time after Charlie's death, Lucien resumed throwing his parties. He and his friends continued to buy art and make art, to drink and reflect. They voted responsibly, they gave to charity, they read the paper assiduously. And while they were basking in their exclusive sunshine, what had happened to the planet? Lucien gazes at his glass of wine, his eyes stinging.

HOMESICK

Nathaniel was eight or nine when his aunt and uncle had come out to the Midwest to visit the family, lustrous and clever and comfortable and humorous and affectionate with one another, in their soft, stylish clothing. They'd brought books with them to read. When they talked to each other—and they habitually did—not only did they take turns, but also, what *one* said followed on what the *other* said. What world could they have come from? What was the world in which beings like his aunt and uncle could exist?

A world utterly unlike his parents', that was for sure—a world of freedom and lightness and beauty and the ardent exchange of ideas and . . . and . . . *fun.*

A great longing rose up in Nathaniel like a flower with a lovely, haunting fragrance. When he was ready, he'd thought—when he was able, when he was worthy, he'd get to the world from which his magic aunt and uncle had once briefly appeared.

The evidence, though, kept piling up that he was not worthy. Because even when he finished school, he simply didn't budge. How unfair it was—his friends had flown off so easily, as if going to New York were nothing at all.

With apparently no effort whatsoever, Madison found himself a job at a fancy New York PR firm. And it seemed that there was a place out there on the trading floor of the Stock Exchange for Amity the instant she finished school. And Lyle had suddenly exhibited an astonishing talent for sound design and engineering, so where else but New York could he reasonably live, either?

Yes, the fact was that only Nathaniel seemed slated to remain behind in their college town. Well, he told himself, his parents were getting on; he would worry, so far away. And he was actually employed as a part-time assistant with an actual architectural firm, whereas in New York the competition, for even the lowliest of such jobs, would be ferocious. And also, he had plenty of time, living where he did, to work on *Passivityman*.

And that's what he told Amity, too, when she'd called one night, four years ago, urging him to take the plunge.

"This is the moment, Nathaniel," she said. "It's time to commit. This oddball, slacker stance is getting kind of old, don't you think, kind of stale. You cannot let your life be ruled by fear any longer."

"'Fear'?" he flinched. "By what fear, exactly, do you happen to believe my life is ruled?"

"Well, I mean, fear of failure, obviously. Fear of mediocrity."

For an instant he thought he might be sick.

"Right," he said. "And why should I fear failure and mediocrity when failure and mediocrity have such august traditions? Anyhow, what's up with you, Amity?"

They'd chatted on for a while, but when they hung up, he felt very, very strange, as if his apartment had slightly changed shape. Amity was right, he'd thought; it was fear that stood between him and the life he ought to be leading.

That was probably the coldest night of the whole, difficult

Millennium. The timid Midwestern sun had basically gone down at the beginning of September; it wouldn't be around much again till May. Black ice glared on the street outside like the cloak of an extra-cruel witch. The sink faucet was dripping into a cracked and stained teacup: *Tick tock tick tock . . .*

What was he *doing*? Once he'd dreamed of designing tranquil and ennobling dwellings, buildings that urged benign relationships, rich inner harmonies; he'd dreamed of meeting fascinating strangers. True, he'd managed to avoid certain pitfalls of middle class adulthood—he wasn't a white collar criminal, for example; he wasn't (at least as far as he knew) a total blowhard. But what was he *actually doing*? His most exciting social contact was the radio. He spent his salaried hours in a cinderblock office building, poring over catalogues of plumbing fixtures. The rest of the day—and the whole evening, too—he sat at the little desk his parents had bought for him when he was in junior high, slaving over *Passivityman*, a comic strip that had made the leap from his college newspaper to his college town's free newspaper, a comic strip that was doted on by whole dozens, the fact was, of stoned undergrads.

He was 24 years old! Soon he'd be 28. In a few more minutes he'd be 35, then 50. Five zero. How had that happened? He was 80! He could feel his vascular system and brain clogging with paste, he was drooling . . .

And if history had anything to teach, it was that he'd be broke when he was 80, too, and that his personal life would still be a disaster.

But wait—Long ago, panic had sent his grandparents and parents scurrying from murderous Europe, with its death camps and pogroms, to the safe harbor of New York. Panic had kept them going as far as the Midwest, where grueling labor enabled them and eventually their children to lead blessedly ordinary lives. And sooner or later, Nathaniel's pounding heart was telling him, that same sure-footed guide, panic, would help him retrace his family's steps, all the way back to Manhattan.

OPPORTUNISM

Blip! Charlie scatters as Lucien's attention wavers from her and the empty space belonging to her is seized by Miss Mueller.

Huh, but what do you know—death *suits* Miss Mueller! In life she was drab, but now she's absolutely radiant with ghoulishness. *You there, Lucien*—the shriek echoes around the gallery—*What are the world's three great religions?*

Zen Buddhism, Jainism, and Sufism, he responds sulkily.

Naughty boy! She cackles flirtatiously. *Bang bang, you're dead*!

THE HALF-LIFE OF PASSIVITY

Passivityman is taking a snooze, his standard response to stress, when the alarm rings. "I'll check it out later, boss," he murmurs.

"You'll check it out *now*, please," his girlfriend and superior, the beautiful Princess Prudence, tells him. "Just put on those grubby corduroys and get out there."

"Aw, is it really *urgent*?" he asks.

"Don't you get it?" she says. "I've been warning you, episode after episode! And now, from his appliance-rich house on the Moon, Captain Corporation has tightened his net of evil around The Planet Earth, and he's dragging it out of orbit! The U.S. Congress is selected by pharmaceutical companies, the State of Israel is run by Christian Fundamentalists, the folks that haul toxic sludge manufacture cattle feed and process burgers, your sources of news and information are edited by a giant mouse, New York City and Christian fundamentalism are holdings of a family in Kuwait—*and all of it's owned by Captain Corporation!*"

Passivityman rubs his eyes and yawns. "Well gosh, Pru, sure—but, like, what am I supposed to do about it?"

"*I* don't know," Princess Prudence says. "It's hardly my job to figure that out, is it? I mean, *you're* the superhero. Just—just—just go out and do something conspicuously lacking in monetary value! Invent some stinky, profit-repelling gloop to pour on stuff. Or, I don't know, whatever. But you'd better do *something*, before it's too late."

"Sounds like it's totally too late already," says Passivityman, reaching for a cigarette.

It was quite a while ago now that Passivityman seemed to throw in the towel. Nathaniel's friends looked at the strip with him and scratched their heads.

"Hm, I don't know, Nathaniel," Amity said. "This episode is awfully complicated. I mean, Passivityman's seeming kind of passive *aggressive*, actually."

"It's not going to be revealed that Passivityman is a double agent, is it?" Madison said. "I mean, what about his undying struggle against corporate-model efficiency?"

"Can Passivityman not be bothered any longer to defend the abject with his greed-repelling Shield of Sloth?" Lyle asked.

"The truth is, I don't really know what's going on with him,"

Nathaniel said. "I was thinking that maybe, unbeknownst to himself, he's come under the thrall of his morally-neutral, transgendering twin, Ambiguityperson."

"Yeah," Madison said. "But I mean, the problem here is that he's just not dealing with the paradox of his own being—he seems kind of *intellectually* passive . . ."

Oh, dear. Poor Passivityman. He was a *tired* old crime-fighter. Nathaniel sighed; it was hard to live the way his superhero lived— constantly vigilant against the premature conclusion, scrupulously rejecting the vulgar ambition, rigorously deferring judgment and action . . . and all for the greater good.

"Huh, well, I guess he's sort of losing his superpowers," Nathaniel said.

The others looked away uncomfortably.

"Oh, it's probably just one of those slumps," Amity said. "I'm sure he'll be back to normal, soon."

But by now, Nathaniel realizes, he's all but stopped trying to work on *Passivityman*.

ALL THIS

Thanks for pointing that out, Miss Mueller. Yes, humanity seems to have reverted by a millennium or so. Goon squads, purporting to represent each of *the world's three great religions*—as they used to be called to 5th graders, and perhaps still so misleadingly are—have deployed themselves all over the map, apparently in hopes of annihilating not only each other, but absolutely everyone, themselves excepted.

Just a few weeks earlier, Lucien was on a plane heading home from Los Angeles, and over the loudspeaker, the pilot requested that all Christians on board raise their hands. The next sickening instants provided more than enough time for conjecture as to who, exactly, was about to be killed—Christians or non-Christians. And then the pilot went on to ask those who had raised their hands to talk about their "faith" with the others.

Well, better him than Rose and Isaac; that would have been two sure heart attacks, right there. And anyhow, why should he be so snooty about religious fanaticism? Stalin managed to kill off over 30 million people in the name of no god at all, and not so very long ago.

At the moment when *all this*—as Lucien thinks of it—began, the moment when a few ordinary looking men carrying box cutters sped past the limits of international negotiation and the frontiers of technology, turning his miraculous city into a nightmare, and hurling the future into a void, Lucien was having his croissant and coffee.

The television was saying something. Lucien wheeled around and stared at it, then turned to look out the window; downtown, black smoke was already beginning to pollute the perfect, silken September morning. On the screen, the ruptured, flaming colossus was shedding veils of tiny black specks.

All circuits were busy, of course; the phone might as well have been a toy. Lucien was trembling as he shut the door of the apartment behind him. His face was wet. Outside, he saw that the sky in the north was still insanely blue.

THE AGE OF DROSS

Well, superpowers were probably a feature of youth, like Wendy's ability to fly around with that creepy Peter Pan. Or maybe they belonged to a loftier period of history. Passivityman's remarkable powers of resistance have been rendered useless; what difference does it make whether he resists or not these days? Everything's going to happen the way it's going to happen. And the superpowers of Nathaniel's friends have been seriously challenged, too. Challenged, or . . . outgrown.

Amity's superpower, her gift for exploiting systemic weaknesses, had taken a terrible beating several years ago when the gold she spun out on the trading floor turned—just like everyone else's—into straw. And subsequently, she plummeted from job to job, through layers of prestige, ending up behind a counter in a fancy department store where she sold overpriced skincare.

Now, of course, the sale of *Inner Beauty Secrets*—her humorous, lightly fictionalized account of her experiences there with her clients—indicates that perhaps her powers are regenerating. But time will tell.

Madison's superpower, an obtuse, patrician equanimity in the face of damning fact, was violently and irremediably terminated one day when a girl arrived at the door asking for him.

"I'm your sister," she told him. "Sorry," Madison said, "I've never seen you before in my life." "Hang on," the girl said. "I'm just getting to that."

For months afterwards, Madison kept everyone awake late into the night repudiating all his former beliefs, his beautiful blue eyes whirling around and his hair standing on end as if he'd stuck his hand into a socket. He quit his lucrative PR job, and denounced the firm's practices in open letters to media watchdog groups (copies to his former boss). The many women who'd been running after him did a fast about-face.

Amity called him a "bitter skeptic;" he called Amity a "dupe." The heated quarrel that followed has tapered off into an uneasy truce, at best.

Lyle's superpower back in school was his spectacular level of aggrievedness and his ability to get anyone at all to feel sorry for him. But later, doing sound with a Paris-based dance group, Lyle met Jahan, who was doing the troupe's lighting.

Jahan is A) as handsome as a prince, B) as charming, as intelligent, as noble in his thoughts, feelings, and actions as a prince, and C) a prince, at least of some attenuated sort. So then no one felt sorry for Lyle at all any longer, and Lyle apparently left the pleasures of even *self*-pity behind him without a second thought.

A while ago, though, Jahan was mistakenly arrested in some sort of sweep near Times Square, and when he was finally released from custody, he moved to London, and now Lyle does nothing but pine, when he can't be in London himself.

"Well, look on the bright side," Nathaniel said. "At least you might get your superpower back."

"You know, Nathaniel—" Lyle said. He looked at Nathaniel for a moment, and then an unfamiliar kindness modified his expression. He patted Nathaniel on the shoulder, and went on his way.

Yikes. Well, so much for Lyle's superpower, obviously.

"It's great that you got to live here for so long, though," Russell is saying.

Nathaniel has the sudden sensation of his whole four years in New York twisting themselves into an arrow, speeding through the air and twanging into the dead center of this evening. "This cannot be happening," he says.

"I think it might really *be* happening, though," Lyle says.

"Fifty percent of respondents say that the event taking place is not occurring," Madison says. "The other fifty percent remain undecided. Clearly, the truth lies somewhere in between."

Soon it might be as if he and Lyle and Madison and Amity had never even lived here. Because this moment is joined to all the other moments they've spent together here, and it's all right now. But soon this moment and all the others will be cut off, in the past, not part of right now at all. Yeah, he and his three friends might all be going their separate ways, come to think of it, once they move out.

CONTINUITY

While the sirens screamed, Lucien had walked against the tide of dazed, smoke-smeared people, down into the fuming cauldron, and when he finally reached the police cordon, his feet aching, he wandered along it for hours, searching for Charlie's nephew, among all the other people who were searching for family, friends, lovers.

Oh, that day! One kept waiting—as if a morning would arrive from before that day to take them all along a different track. One kept waiting for that shattering day to unhappen, so that the real—the intended—future, the one that had been implied by the past, could unfold. Hour after hour, month after month, waiting for that day to not have happened. But it had happened. And now it was always going to have happened.

Most likely on the very mornings that first Rose and then Isaac had disembarked at Ellis Island, each clutching some remnant of the world they were never to see again, Lucien was being wheeled in his pram through the genteel world, a few miles uptown, of brownstones.

The city, more than his body, contained his life. His life! The schools he had gone to as a child, the market where his mother had bought the groceries, the park where he had played with his classmates, the restaurants where he had courted Charlie, the various apartments they'd lived in, the apartments of their friends, the gallery, the newsstand on the corner, the dry cleaner's, the grocery store, his local restaurants . . . The things he did in the course of the day, year after year, the people he encountered.

A sticky layer of crematorium ash settled over the whole of Matsumoto's neighborhood, even inside, behind closed windows, as thick in places as turf, and water was unavailable for a time. Nathaniel and his friends all stayed elsewhere, of course, for a few weeks. When it became possible, Lucien sent crews down to Matsumoto's loft to scour the place and restore the art.

FAREWELL

A memorandum hangs in Mr. Matsumoto's lobby that appeared several months ago when freakish blackouts were rolling over the city.

Emergency Tips from the Management urges residents to

assemble a Go Bag, in the event of an evacuation, as well as an In-Home Survival Kit. Among items to include: a large amount of cash in small denominations, water and non-perishable foods such as granola bars, a wind-up radio, warm clothing and sturdy walking shoes, unscented bleach and an eyedropper for purifying water, plastic sheeting and duct tape, a whistle, a box cutter.

Also recommended is a Household Disaster Plan and the practicing of emergency drills.

A hand-lettered sign next to the elevator says Think Twice.

Twenty-eight years old, no superhero, a job that just *might* lead down to a career in underground architecture, a vanishing apartment, a menacing elevator . . . Maybe he should view Mr. Matsumoto's return as an opportunity, and regroup. Maybe he should *do* something—take matters in hand. Maybe he should go try to find Delphine, for example.

But how? He hasn't heard from her, and she could be anywhere now; she'd mentioned Bucharest, she'd mentioned Havana, she'd mentioned Shanghai, she'd mentioned Istanbul . . .

He'd met her at one his uncle's parties. There was the usual huge roomful of people wearing strangely-pleated black clothes, like the garments of a somber devotional sect, and there she was in electric blue taffeta, amazingly tall and narrow, lazy and nervous, like an electric bluebell.

She favored men nearly twice Nathaniel's age and millions of times richer, but for a while she let Nathaniel come over to her apartment and play her his favorite CDs. They drank perfumey infusions from chipped porcelain cups, or vodka. Delphine could become thrillingly drunk, and she smoked, letting long columns of ash form on her tarry, unfiltered cigarettes. One night, when he lost his keys, she let him come over and sleep in her bed while she went out, and when the sky fell, she actually let him sleep on her floor for a week.

Her apartment was filled with puffy, silky little sofas, and old, damaged mirrors and tarnished candlesticks, and tall vases filled with slightly wilting flowers. It smelled like powder and tea and cigarettes and her Abyssinian cats, which prowled the savannas of the white, longhaired rugs or posed on the marble mantelpiece.

Delphine's father was Armenian and he lived in Paris, which according to Delphine was a bore. Her mother was Chilean. Delphine's English had been acquired at a boarding school in Kent for dull-witted rich girls and castaways, like herself, from everywhere.

She spoke many languages, she was self-possessed and beautiful and fascinating. She could have gone to live anywhere. And she had come, like Nathaniel, to New York.

"But look at it now," she'd raged. Washington was dropping bombs on Afghanistan and then Iraq, and every few weeks there was a flurry of alerts in kindergarten colors indicating the likelihood of terrorist attacks — Yellow, orange, red, *duck!*

"Do you know how I get the real news here?" Delphine said. "I get it in taxis, from the drivers! And how do they get it? From their friends and relatives who are over there. The drivers sit around at the airport, swapping information, and they can tell you *anything*. But do you ask? Or sometimes I talk to my friends in Europe. Do you know what they're saying about you over there?"

"Please don't say 'you,' Delphine," he had said faintly.

"Oh, yes, here it's not like stuffy old Europe, where everything is stifled by tradition and trauma. Here you're able to speak freely, within reason, of course, and isn't it wonderful that you all happen to want to say exactly what they want you to say? Do you know how many people you're killing over there? No, how would you? Good, just keep your eyes closed, panic, don't ask any questions, and you can speak freely about whatever you like. And if you have any suspicious looking neighbors, be sure to tell the police. You had everything here, everything, and you threw it all away in one second."

She was so beautiful; he'd gazed at her as if he were already remembering her. "Please don't say 'you,'" he murmured again.

"Poor Nathaniel," she said. "This place is nothing now but a small-minded, mean-spirited provincial town."

THE AGE OF DIGITAL REASONING

One/two. On/off. The plane crashes/doesn't crash.

That plane he had taken from LA didn't crash. It wasn't used as a missile to blow anything up, and not even one passenger was shot or stabbed. Nothing happened. So, what was the problem? What was the difference between having been on that flight and having been on any other flight in his life?

Oh, what's the point of thinking about death all the time! Think about it or not, you die. Besides—and here's something that sure hasn't changed—you don't have to do it more than once. And as you don't have to do it *less* than once, either, you might as well do it on the plane. Maybe there's no special problem these days. Maybe the problem is just that he's old.

Or maybe his nephew's is the last generation that will remember what it had once felt like to blithely assume there would be a future—

at least a future like the one that had been implied by the past they'd all been familiar with.

But the future actually ahead of them, it's now obvious, had itself been implied by a past; and the terrible day that pointed them toward that future had been prepared for a long, long time, though it had been prepared behind a curtain.

It was as if there had been a curtain, a curtain painted with the map of the earth, its oceans and continents, with Lucien's delightful city. The planes struck, tearing through the curtain of that blue September morning, exposing the dark world that lay right behind it, of populations ruthlessly exploited, inflamed with hatred, and tired of waiting for change to happen by.

The stump of the ruined tower continued to smolder far into the fall, and an unseasonable heat persisted. When the smoke lifted, all kinds of other events, which had been prepared behind a curtain, too, were revealed. Flags waved in the brisk air of fear, files were requisitioned from libraries and hospitals, droning helicopters hung over the city, and heavily armed policemen patrolled the parks. Meanwhile, one read that executives had pocketed the savings of their investors and the pensions of their employees.

The wars in the East were hidden behind a thicket of language: *Patriotism, democracy, loyalty, freedom*—the words bounced around, changing purpose, as if they were made out of some funny plastic. What did they actually refer to? It seemed that they all might refer to money.

Were the sudden power outages and spiking level of unemployment related? And what was causing them? The newspapers seemed for the most part to agree that the cause of both was terrorism. But lots of people said they were both the consequence of corporate theft. It was certainly all beyond Lucien! Things that had formerly appeared to be distinct, or even at odds, now seemed to have been smoothly blended, to mutual advantage. Provocation and retribution, arms manufacture and statehood, oil and war, commerce and dogma— and the spinning planet seemed to be boiling them all together at the center of the earth into a poison syrup. Enemies had soared towards each other from out of the past to unite in a joyous fireball; planes had sheared through the heavy, painted curtain and from the severed towers an inexhaustible geyser had erupted.

Styles of pets revolved rapidly, as if the city's residents were searching for a type of animal that would express a stance appropriate to the horrifying assault, which for all anyone knew was only the first of many.

For a couple of months everyone was walking cute, perky things. Then Lucien saw snarling hounds everywhere and the occasional boa constrictor draped around its owner's shoulders. After that, it was tiny, trembling dogs that traveled in purses and pockets.

New York had once been the threshold of an impregnable haven, then the city had become in an instant the country's open wound, and now it was the occasion—the pretext!—for killing and theft and legislative horrors all over the world. The air stank from particulate matter—chemicals and asbestos and blood and scorched bone. People developed coughs and strange rashes.

What should be done, and to whom? Almost any word, even between friends, could ignite a sheet of flame. What were the bombings for? First one imperative was cited and then another; the rationales shifted hastily to cover successive gaps in logic. Bills were passed containing buried provisions, and loopholes were triumphantly discovered — alarming elasticities or rigidities in this law or that. One was sick of trying to get a solid handle on the stream of pronouncements — it was like endlessly trying to sort little bits of paper into stacks when a powerful fan was on.

Friends in Europe and Asia sent him clippings about his own country. *What's all this*, they asked — secret arrests and detentions, his president capering about in military uniform, crazy talk of pre-emptive nuclear strikes? Why were they releasing a big science fiction horror movie over there, about the emperor of everything everywhere, for which the whole world was required to buy tickets? What on earth was going on with them all, why were they all so silent? Why did they all seem so confused?

How was he to know, Lucien thought. If his foreign friends had such great newspapers, why didn't *they* tell *him*!

No more smiles from strangers on the street! Well, it was reasonable to be frightened; everyone had seen what those few men were able do with the odds and ends in their pockets. The heat lifted, and then there was unremitting cold. No one lingered to joke and converse in the course of their errands, but instead hurried irritably along, like people with bad consciences.

And always in front of you now was the sight that had been hidden by the curtain, of all those irrepressibly, murderously, angry people.

Private life shrank to nothing. All one's feelings had been absorbed by an arid wasteland—policy, strategy, goals . . . One's past, one's future, one's ordinary daily pleasures were like dusty little curios on a shelf.

Lucien continued defiantly throwing his parties, but as the murky wars dragged on, he stopped. It was impossible to have fun or to want to have fun. It was one thing to have fun if the sun was shining generally, quite another thing to have fun if it was raining blood everywhere but on your party. What did he and his friends really have in common, anyway? Maybe nothing more than their level of privilege.

In restaurants and cafes all over the city, people seemed to have changed. The good-hearted, casually wasteful festival was over. In some places the diners were sullen and dogged, as if they felt accused of getting away with something.

In other places, the gaiety was cranked up to the level of completely unconvincing hysteria. For a long miserable while, in fact, the city looked like a school play about war profiteering. The bars were overflowing with very young people from heaven only knew where, in hideous, ludicrously showy clothing, spending massive amounts of money on green, pink, and orange cocktails, and laughing at the top of their lungs, as if at filthy jokes.

No, not like a school play—like a movie, though the performances and the direction were crude. The loud, ostensibly carefree young people appeared to be extras recruited from the suburbs, and yet sometime in the distant future, people seeing such a movie might think oh yes; that was a New York that existed once, say, at the end of the Millennium.

It was Lucien's city, Lucien's times, and yet what he appeared to be living in wasn't the actual present—it was an inaccurate representation of the *past*. True, it looked something like the New York that existed before *all this* began, but Lucien remembered, and he could see: the costumes were not quite right, the hairstyles were not quite right, the gestures and the dialogue were not quite right.

Oh. Yes. Of course none of it was quite right—the movie was a *propaganda* movie. And now it seems that the propaganda movie has done its job; things, in a grotesque sense, are back to normal.

Money is flowing a bit again, most of the flags have folded up, those nerve-wracking terror alerts have all but stopped, the kids in the restaurants have calmed down, no more rolling blackouts, and the dogs on the street encode no particular messages. Once again, people are concerned with getting on with their lives. Once again, the curtain has dropped.

Except that people seem a little bit nervous, a little uncomfortable, a little wary. Because you can't help sort of knowing that what you're seeing is only the curtain. And you can't help guessing what might be going on behind it.

THE FARTHER IN THE PAST THINGS ARE, THE BIGGER THEY BECOME

Nathaniel remembers more and more rather than less and less vividly the visit of his uncle and aunt to the Midwest during his childhood.

He'd thought his Aunt Charlie was the most beautiful woman he'd ever seen. And for all he knows, she really was. He never saw her after that one visit; by the time he came to New York and acquainted his adult self with Uncle Lucien she had been dead for a long time. She would still have been under 50 when she died—crushed, his mother had once, in a mood, implied, by the weight of her own pretensions.

His poor mother! She had cooked, cleaned, and fretted for . . . months, it had seemed, in preparation for that visit of Uncle Lucien and Aunt Charlie. And observing in his memory the four grownups, Nathaniel can see an awful lot of white knuckles.

He remembers his mother picking up a book Aunt Charlie had left lying on the kitchen table, glancing at it and putting it back down with a tiny shrug and a lifted eyebrow. "You don't approve?" Aunt Charlie said, and Nathaniel is shocked to see, in his memory, that she is tense.

His mother, having gained the advantage, makes another bitter little shrug. "I'm sure it's over my head," she says.

When the term of the visit came to an end, they dropped Uncle Lucien and Aunt Charlie at the airport. His brother was driving, too fast. Nathaniel can hear himself announcing in his child's piercing voice, *"I want to live in New York like Uncle Lucien and Aunt Charlie!"* His exile's heart was brimming, but it was clear from his mother's profile that she was braced for an execution.

"Slow *down*, Bernie!" his mother said, but Bernie hadn't. "Big shot," she muttered, though it was unclear at whom this was directed—whether at his brother or himself or his father, or his Uncle Lucien, or at Aunt Charlie herself.

BACK TO NORMAL

Do dogs have to fight sadness as tirelessly as humans do? They seem less involved with retrospect, less involved in dread and anticipation. Animals other than humans appear to be having a more profound experience of the present. But who's to say? Clearly their feelings are intense, and maybe grief and anxiety darken all their days. Maybe that's why they've acquired their stripes and polka dots and fluffiness—to cheer themselves up.

Poor old Earth, an old sponge, a honeycomb of empty mineshafts and dried wells. While he and his friends were wittering on, the planet underfoot had been looted. The waterways glint with weapons-grade plutonium, sneaked on barges between one wrathful nation and another, the polar ice caps melt, Venice sinks.

In the horrible old days in Europe when Rose and Isaac were hunted children, it must have been pretty clear to them how to behave, minute by minute. Men in jackboots? Up to the attic!

But even during that time when it was so dangerous to speak out, to act courageously, heroes emerged. Most of them died fruitlessly, of course, and unheralded. But now there are even monuments to some of them, and information about such people is always coming to light.

Maybe there really is no problem, maybe everything really is back to normal, and maybe the whole period will sink peacefully away, to be remembered only by scholars. But if it should end in catastrophe, whom will the monuments of the future commemorate?

Today, all day long, Lucien has seen the president's vacant, stricken expression staring from the ubiquitous television screens.

He seemed to be talking about positioning weapons in space, colonizing the moon.

Open your books to page 167, class, Miss Mueller shrieks. *What do you see?*

Lucien sighs.

The pages are thin and sort of shiny. The illustrations are mostly black and white.

This one's a photograph of a statue, an emperor, apparently, wearing his stone toga and his stone wreath. The real people, the living people, mill about just beyond the picture's borders, but Lucien knows more or less what they look like—he's seen illustrations of them, too. He knows what a viaduct is and what the ancient Romans wore and that they had a code of law from which his country's own is derived. Are the people hidden by the picture frightened? Do they hear the stones working themselves loose, the temples and houses and courts beginning to crumble?

Out the window, the sun is just a tiny, tiny bit higher today than it was at this exact instant yesterday. After school today, he and Robbie Stern will go play soccer in the park. In another month it will be bright and warm.

PARADISE

So, Mr. Matsumoto will be coming back, and things seem pretty much as they did when he left. The apartment is clean, the cats are healthy, the art is undamaged, and the view from the terrace is exactly the same, except there's that weird, blank spot where the towers used to stand.

"Open the next?" Madison says, holding up a bottle of champagne. "Strongly agree, agree, undecided, disagree, strongly disagree."

"Strongly agree," Lyle says.

"Thanks," Amity says.

"Okay," Russell says. "I'm in."

Nathaniel shrugs and holds out his glass.

Madison pours. "Polls indicate that 100 percent of the American public approves heavy drinking," he says.

"Oh, God, Madison," Amity says. "Can't we ever just *drop* it? Can't we ever just have a nice time?"

Madison looks at her for a long moment. "Drop what?" he says, evenly.

But no one wants to get into *that*.

When Nathaniel was in his last year at college, his father began to suffer from heart trouble. It was easy enough for Nathaniel to come home on the weekends, and he'd sit with his father, gazing out the window as the autumnal light gilded the dry grass and the fallen leaves glowed.

His father talked about his own time at school, working night and day, the pride his parents had taken in him, the first college student in their family.

Over the years Nathaniel's mother and father had grown gentler with one another and with him. Sometimes after dinner and the dishes, they'd all go out for a treat. Nathaniel would wait, a scalding pity weakening his bones, while his parents debated worriedly over their choices, as if nobody ever had before or would ever have again the opportunity to eat ice cream.

Just last night, he dreamed about Delphine, a beautiful champagne-style dream, full of love and beauty—a weird, high quality love, a feeling he doesn't remember ever having had in his waking life—a pure, wholehearted, shining love.

It hangs around him still, floating through the air out on the terrace—fragrant, shimmering, fading.

WAITING

The bell is about to ring. Closing his book Lucien hears the thrilling crash as the bloated empire tumbles down.

Gold star, Lucien! Miss Mueller cackles deafeningly, and then she's gone.

Charlie's leaving, too. Lucien lifts his glass; she glances back across the thin, inflexible divide.

From farther than the moon she sees the children of some distant planet study pictures in their text: there's Rose and Isaac at their kitchen table, Nathaniel out on Mr. Matsumoto's terrace, Lucien alone in the dim gallery—and then the children turn the page.